LUZIA HAGENMÜLLER

YOUNG, IN THE MIDDLE OF LIFE AND A MEMBER OF INNER WHEEL

Books on Demand GmbH

YOUNG, IN THE MIDDLE OF LIFE AND A MEMBER OF INNER WHEEL

5 Statements

Publisher: LUZIA HAGENMÜLLER

Translated from the German
by Michael Hogan

Thanks

My great thanks go to my Inner Wheel friends, Dr Mechtild Brüggestrat, Elisabeth Dörner, Christin Lens, Britta Trumann and Elke Weinhold for their speeches made during the 65th district conference of the 89th District of IIW on November 6, 2010, in Berlin and their kind permission to reproduce them in this book.
My special thanks go to Michael Hogan, who was so kind to translate this book from the German.

Copyright © 2012 Luzia Hagenmüller

Printed and published by
Books on Demand GmbH, Norderstedt, Germany, www.bod.com
ISBN 9 783848 214211

Original title: Jung, mitten im Leben und Mitglied bei Inner Wheel
Copyright © 2011 Luzia Hagenmüller

Books on Demand GmbH, Norderstedt, Germany, www.bod.com
ISBN 9 783842 363649

The Book

Five young, in midlife members of the Inner Wheel Club in the 89th District of the International Inner Wheel describe their motivation, experiences of and wishes from their Inner Wheel membership from the viewpoint of their situation in life.

The Publisher

Luzia Hagenmüller, district chairman of the 89th District of the International Inner Wheel in 2010-2011 and President of the Inner Wheel Club Hamburg in 2007-2008.
She worked as a teacher up to the birth of her four children, then devoted herself fully to "family management". After her children grew up she took up a range of honorary positions and is today active in the Inner Wheel.
She has lived in several cities. This means there is a special meaning for her in the quotation from Kurt Tucholsky **"Friendship – that is home for me."** She selected this as the theme for her year as district chairman.

Contents

Introduction: Luzia Hagenmüller   11

Statements: Dr. Mechtild Brüggestrat   15

                Britta Trumann   21

                Christin Lens   27

                Elke Weinhold   33

                Elisabeth Dörner   41

Appendix: What is Inner Wheel ?   47

                International Inner Wheel

LUZIA HAGENMÜLLER

District chairman 2010-2011
International Inner Wheel, District 89

President of the Inner Wheel Club Hamburg 2007-2008

Friendship – That is home for me. (Kurt Tucholsky)

Introduction

One point on the agenda of the 65th district conference of the 89th District of the **International Inner Wheel** on November 6, 2010, in Berlin was:

Young members for Inner Wheel.

Attracting young women to membership is of great importance if Inner Wheel is to stay in tune with the times and retain the charm of a women's club spanning generations.

You often hear that young women and those standing middle in life have little interest in joining a service club like **Inner Wheel**. On the one hand, the needs of the family or profession leave little spare time to regularly participate in club life.

Meanwhile, there is also great attraction to the new forms of communication which provide strong competition to traditional club life.

The question can be asked: In the age of Facebook, Twitter and other virtual friendship communities and networks, what is the interest of Inner Wheel to young and middle aged women? A laptop is no use for the sort of friendships made with Inner Wheel.

Inner Wheel does not offer the business network provided by other women's clubs or by Rotary. Yet there are many highly-qualified women in Inner Wheel. These include women with senior positions in professional life and who play leading roles in social work. The title doctor and even professor are often heard.

So what makes Inner Wheel attractive?

Perhaps because you have the opportunity to move away from the egoistic values which are today so dominant in the professional world and even in private social life.

Inner Wheel does not make judgements according to income, influence, measurable performance or social position – but instead judges personal social service and community commitment.

This commitment can be illustrated in ways some people would not regard as spectacular: Helping to organise a charity event or perhaps visiting a home for the elderly at Christmas to speak to the people and drink a coffee with them. It could also be seen in the support of international education projects such as the Inner Wheel project entitled Education for Girls in Bolivia.

For Inner Wheel, living values such as friendship, willingness to help others, empathy, respect and tolerance are of great importance. These values reach beyond your own club and reach beyond your own country – they are global. We members of the Inner Wheel want to face this challenge.

Five young and in midlife members of the 89th district of the International Inner Wheel described their motivation, experiences of and wishes from the Inner Wheel during the 65th district conference. You will discover their ideas in the following pages.

DR. MECHTILD BRÜGGESTRAT

President 2010-2011
IWC Hamburg-South

True friendship not feigned friendship

My name is Mechtild Brüggestrat. I am 53 years old, married and have two children aged 16 and 19 years. I studied economic science and achieved my PhD. For many years I worked as the head of the branch office of a business consulting company. When we moved to Hamburg in 2001 my professional life changed. I qualified as a natural health therapist and for the past four years I have worked as a self-employed natural health therapist with my own practice in Heimfeld in Hamburg.

I joined the Inner Wheel Club Hamburg-South when I was aged 45. I have served as club secretary, was treasurer for three years and was most recently president. The IWC Hamburg-South has 46 members and has a diversified structure with many young Inner Wheelers. The oldest member is 89 and the youngest is 38 years old, 40 % of the members are under 60.

What interested me and motivated me to join Inner Wheel?

When my family and I moved from the Ruhr to Hamburg in 2001 and we took part in the activities of my husband's Rotary Club, I found the club life was rather different from the style I had been used to. In the Rotary Club Gelsenkirchen-North club life was characterised by close cooperation between Rotary men and their wives - organising joint bazaars, baking waffles, visiting homes for the elderly and so on. Here in Hamburg that was not the case. In the past I had greatly enjoyed my commitment to personal service work. So I had great interest in finding out more about the IWC Hamburg-South and became a member in 2003. A major reason for my membership was my interest in a commitment to social work for the needy.

Friendship is another aspect. When I moved to the wonderful city of Hamburg in 2001, I knew no one. So the opportunity to make new friendships through Inner Wheel was a great enrichment. The extremely stimulating and comprehensive offer of joint activities and the open and welcoming way new members were accepted in the club offered many opportunities to find new friends. During the very first club trip it became clear to me that even more was offered alongside the interesting meetings, joint museum visits and many private invitations. This was the encounters between young and old, the conversations spanning generations and the warm-hearted welcome, especially from the older Inner Wheelers. This left a very strong impression and also promoted a rapid integration in the club. It was a personally enriching experience to hear the older members describe their life stories, to consider what they had done and compare this with the very different lift plans of the younger members. This was a living piece of women's history.

True friendship - not feigned friendship, simply what you are and without sham. Everyone comes into conversation with everyone, that is what I value greatly at Inner Wheel. Friendship and contacts which have not been generated by your profession, sport or children. Friendship is instead created under the framework of a joint commitment to friendship, willingness to help others and a wish for more international understanding. This is a moving experience at Inner Wheel - again and again.

Inner Wheel is especially for working women a place where friendships can be made and maintained without the pressure of competition, without any joint professional background. After a long day you can simply relax and leave the stress of work behind you. What counts is the human factor, the relaxed atmosphere and the pleasure from the joint activities.

When I was preparing this presentation, it became ever more clearer to me that the reasons for making a commitment to Inner Wheel are very wide ranging and it is important for every club to simply accept new friends as they are. This is an important factor to take on new members and integrate them. Taking over the mentoring of a new member can also assist integration. It is especially important for young Inner Wheelers to hold an office as quickly as possible. All the offices can be mastered and the best and fastest way of gaining a true view and feeling of Inner Wheel life is by handling an office.

What is the future of Inner Wheel?

The future course looks like becoming very diverse. There are clubs in large cities and in rural areas which have difficulties in finding new members. Meetings in the evening permit both working women and mothers with children to take part. In addition there is also the option of accepting extraordinary members. When we have stands at events we are often spoken to by women who are interested in our work and would also like to become involved in personal service work but who also have no Rotary background. I will leave open the question whether our future lies in a de-coupling from the Rotary connection.

BRITTA TRUMANN

President 2010-2011
IWC Stormarn

It must be possible to work and attend one Inner Wheel meeting a month!

* Quick introduction
Britta Trumann IWC Stormarn
Happily married for 30 years
One daughter: Conny, 32 years young

Luzia Hagenmüller visited our club in Ahrensburg in September and we started discussing "young members" for the Inner Wheel. Naturally I feel very flattered that I can talk about this issue here. With 48 years I am among the "middle ages".

For me everything started "somewhat" earlier – Why not also consider membership of Inner Wheel? Shortly after my husband Michael was accepted in the Rotary Club Bad Oldesloe in 2003, the then president of the IWC Stormarn spoke to me about joining.

I felt myself very honoured but initially asked for some time to think. Because when I do something I do it properly!

My work then and today involves a 40-hour week in an IT corporate consultancy. Even to reach my workplace, I need at least two additional hours in the car. This means that 50 hours a week are fixed in the work plan. But an especially pleasurable feature of this is that I work together with my husband (and have done so for 23 years!!) and so we spend a lot of time together.

My resolution: It must be possible to have a job and have time to attend one Inner Wheel meeting a month! In addition, I already knew many of the wives through Rotary and had already encountered their warm-hearted way with each other.

So in January 2004 I was warmly welcomed into "my" club. I immediately enjoyed the pleasant friendship, the cordial atmosphere. I quickly realised – the meetings are much more than just a gathering!

It was especially at our bazaars, the meetings with our Danish friendship club and the clothing market which generated happy hours again and again.

The joint activities with the Rotarians and the youth organisation Rotaract in the town and spa park festivals may have generated extra work, but they also gave me great pleasure and deepened friendships. They gave me a wonderful chance to switch off from the pressures of daily life and afterwards in the evening I fell asleep tired but happy! It is simply marvellous to achieve something together and then use the money you have raised to help someone in need!

I must be honest: After a hard day's work it could naturally be that I was tired and did not really want to go to the meeting - but my sense of duty won! And every time it did me good.

I have now been a member of "my" Inner Wheel Club Stormarn for almost seven years of which I have held an office for five years! I was initially the treasurer of the then newly-established promotional society. Later I also became treasurer of the club and this year I am accompanying my club as president through the Inner Wheel year.

My motto is a theme dear to my heart "Maintain and deepen existing friendships." This goes hand in hand with the theme of our district president!

Mrs Hagenmüller, you also asked me what suggestions I would regard as an improvement to Inner Wheel. My answer is quite simple: The Inner Wheel year must have more hours. I have so many ideas for "my year" and the time goes by much too quickly....

But I am certain: If you plan and really want to achieve something, you will achieve it! And this also creates great pleasure and deepens friendships.

CHRISTIN LENS

Vice president 2010 – 2011
IWC Niederelbe

"No one can do everything – everyone can do something – together we can reach our goal."

That is my theme for the coming year when I will become president of the IWC Niederelbe.

I am Christin Lens, 45 years old, housewife and married for 20 years to a Dutchman who has been a member of the Rotary Club in Stade for 10 years. We have had four children together and they are aged 20, 18, 16 and 11 years.

Six years ago in January 2004 when I was 39 years old, an Inner Wheeler was talking to me during a Rotary ladies' outing. She vividly described Inner Wheel and told me about individual projects and the friendships inside the club.

Finally she smiled and said: "You know of course why I am telling you all this. If you like, come to our meeting next month!"

Quite honestly I had never heard of Inner Wheel although my husband had been a member of Rotary at that time for years. But I had a wish to become more involved in personal social service work. I had worked in nurseries and schools for some years and had also led a children's group in the church for two years. The community of like-minded women, who show commitment to help those in society less fortunate than themselves - and who also have great fun and pleasure in their work – was a new challenge for me.

At first I had reservations. My youngest son was just about to start school, a daughter was still in the infants' school and the two others were in their 7th and 8th school years. I was responsible for supervising the children from midday to the late afternoon. This meant especially driving the children to school events, sport or confirmation class etc. and that for four children. Most of us know that there are too few hours in the day!

Despite this I wanted to visit a meeting. My husband supported me in the whole idea. So I visited three meetings before I decided to join the club.

From the very beginning I was received with openness and friendship. The members treated each other in a trustful, tolerant way and I valued the willingness to help, the friendship and the commitment to personal social service. The experience of the older Inner Wheelers strengthens the confidence in your own abilities and if you have questions they are always at your side with advice and help.

In our club, every member decides themselves how much time they can invest in Inner Wheel. Those working have to put their job first. For the Inner Wheelers with children, the family gets top priority. So they cannot take part in the three-day club trips, which they greatly regret. Outings or visits in the afternoons are also difficult for them to organise.

For me this was not such an issue. This is because firstly my mother lives nearby and is ready to jump in and help at any time. Secondly my husband is an all-round talent who along with his job can also take over caring for the children for several days in a row without the housework coming to a stop.

The Inner Wheelers who have been members for a long time work to promote their friendships both internally (joint fireside evenings, club travels, joint activities) and externally (participation in friendship meetings, club visits and Dinner Wheel). The younger members come to the meetings and participate in various sales events held in the morning when the children are in the nursery or school.

An Inner Wheel friend made this comment to me: "In earlier days, when my mother joined Inner Wheel, it was sometimes easier. You could simply take the children with you. It did not matter if you took them to one of the joint activities or to a bicycle tour. All the women were about the same age and the children knew each other."

Today, the younger Inner Wheelers quickly get a bad conscience if they take their children with them and this was not expressly indicated in advance, for example in the minutes.

Conclusion: They would welcome the opportunity to take their children to events more often!

Another great advantage is holding an evening meeting once a month and not only midday and afternoon meetings as in other clubs.

We have great fun raising money for good causes, without gain for ourselves, by starting projects to help people in need. We are not only interested in the enjoyable socialising, but also in the interesting speeches, readings and ego reports.

In the course of time you also gain more contacts with other clubs and exchange visits can take place which can also create new friendships.

New, young members could be attracted via Rotary and Rotaract. Or members could bring their friends who could become extraordinary members. When sales events are held, interested women could be shown our Inner Wheel leaflet. If their interest is stimulated further they could be invited to a meeting so that they can convince themselves about our work.

For me it is a pleasure to be a member of the IWC Niederelbe. For me it is a personal enrichment. It has strengthened my self confidence and am able to take on greater challenges with equanimity.

ELKE WEINHOLD

President 2010-2011
IWC Herzogtum Lauenburg

The idea behind Inner Wheel convinced me

My name is Elke Weinhold. I am currently the president of the IWC Herzogtum Lauenburg. Our district chairman Luzia Hagenmüller asked me to make a short presentation answering the following five questions:

1. How old were you when you joined Inner Wheel?

When I joined Inner Wheel I was 47years old.

2. Why did you join Inner Wheel?

Only three years ago Inner Wheel meant very little to me. For me it was an association of women who for example visited patients who were alone in hospitals and had no one else to see. I had heard about the club from an earlier Inner Wheeler who was a member of the former Inner Wheel Club Oldenburg/Holstein. She was the first Inner Wheeler I can remember talking directly to about the club.

Later in spring 2008, our future founding president Christine Knoth asked me if I would be interested in helping set up an Inner Wheel club. I spontaneously accepted. I did not have precise knowledge about Inner Wheel but I saw a chance to help influence the shape of a newly-established Service club.

I gathered my first concrete knowledge about Inner Wheel during an information event on June 16, 2008, with the person then responsible for the club establishment, Claudia Hohrein. She told us about social welfare activities, speeches and the organisation of Inner Wheel. As the main focus point she stressed the friendship between Inner Wheelers and told us about how Inner Wheel had helped support her in a crisis in her life. This aspect of her description appeared to me at the time to be of lesser importance. For me it was more important to become active in social welfare work with others. The idea of Inner Wheel convinced 14 of those attending so that on the same evening we established the IWC Herzogtum Lauenburg. I stood and was elected as vice president so that I could work in the managing committee and help influence the form of the club from the very beginning.

Those were my reasons to become an Inner Wheeler two and a half years ago. If you include the 14 days in the part year from June 16 to June 30, 2008, I am now in my fourth Inner Wheel year and have taken part in the district conference five times. I have also taken part in the vice presidents' meetings in Cuxhaven and Hamburg. I learnt very much about Inner Wheel at these meetings. Naturally these were extremely hectic years for our district. For example, only five days after establishing the club, Christine Knoth and I attended the exciting district conference in Breitenburg where we learnt much about the organisation. In addition, I gathered many stimulating ideas for our club at all the events I attended. In conclusion, I can say that I have never for one day regretted my decision of June 16, 2008.

3. What is interesting for you at Inner Wheel?

As a member of Inner Wheel I am a part of a network spanning the whole world. You get a simply fantastic feeling when you think that when you are selling cakes or game sausages other women in America, Japan or India are undertaking the same sort of fund-raising activities to help the education of young girls in Bolivia.

Because of my work in a service club like Inner Wheel I have the opportunity to make something happen, often with relatively small resources, through joint action. Otherwise these things would not have happened.

There are many possibilities to help people by undertaking unpaid, honorary work and I had done this many times before my membership of Inner Wheel. But over the years I have had the experience that it is always the same people who come forward when help is needed for the children's bazaar at the nursery or sport club, when cakes need to be baked for the school or when someone must take a day off work when the class has to be escorted to a Christmas pantomime etc. Even though I had a lot of fun by helping out at such events, I started experiencing a feeling of frustration recently when I started to think how many people simply took such help for granted.

My social commitment to Inner Wheel is different from such other activities. We do not feel a moral obligation to help out in such events because of the sure knowledge that they will not take place unless outside help is given. Instead we think ourselves about the events we would like to stage or can and want to support.

I would like to stress a thought from Luzia Hagenmüller which she expressed during a visit to our club: You get more pleasure from making joint commitment to a good cause than just writing out a cheque for someone in need.

So I now come to the aspect which nowadays is the most important reason for my pleasure gained from my membership of Inner Wheel: The friendship. Our Inner Wheel Club now has 28 members, three of whom only joined a few days ago. I can only say of the other 24 that they are my friends and I am convinced that I will also be able to say this soon about our three new members. I did not know many of these friends earlier as our club covers an area with three Rotary Clubs which even belong to different districts (1890 and 1940). Through Inner Wheel I have also made many friendships beyond our club and met interesting women. At the first district conference only a few days after our club was established, Christine Knoth and I experienced the warm welcome into the Inner Wheel family. This could also be experienced by all of our club friends who had the opportunity to meet other Inner Wheelers at the charter celebrations.

4. How can you reconcile job, children and Inner Wheel?

In my belief this is primarily a question of the planning and organisation and setting of priorities. I am a judge and I have two daughters aged 10 and 18 years. From the beginning I made certain that on my meeting days (generally once a week) someone was available if one of the children became ill and needed looking after. So I have never missed a meeting because of a child being ill. On the other hand my profession makes it possible – and this is one reason why I chose it – to leave work immediately on a day when I have no court session or meeting. I can break off work and go home immediately or stay at home if a child needs me. This is because I have the freedom to organise my own work. In addition I always have a deputy ready to spring in for me if I need to stay at home but also have to handle an unplanned professional commitment, eg a custody order. The appointments and events involving Inner Wheel are generally known well in advance and so can be planned. I can then make sure that my young daughter is not alone.

5. How can young women be attracted to Inner Wheel?

Women must be told that the great network in Inner Wheel can often make problems easier to solve. For example, the difficulties in a nursery or school can be shared with non-mothers or former mothers and joint help achieved.

The women must be told that it is great fun to be jointly active in personal social service in Inner Wheel because your own projects and ideas can be developed.

The women must be told that in Inner Wheel you can hear interesting presentations and speeches. Perhaps this is similar to a season ticket for all the plays in a theatre: This means you will see and hear about themes which you had previously not been very interested in and without Inner Wheel would not have heard about.

The women must be told that you can make many friendships at Inner Wheel – including at an international level.

The women must be told that Inner Wheel is different from other service clubs such as Rotary or the Soroptimists because there is no qualification requirement in terms of your work or your education. This means that on the one had no woman will be asked if she wants to be a member just because the club would gain in its image from her membership. She is only asked because it is wished to win her as a friend. On the other hand, no one joins or is asked to join Inner Wheel because it promises some sort of advantage in professional or social status. The membership of Inner Wheel promises only something for yourself and the opportunity to do something good.

At our founding meeting, our friend Gerda Jung said: When there are 12 or more women who want to jointly do something good, then they should set up this sort of club. This happened for us and I hope it will happen many more times elsewhere.

ELISABETH DÖRNER

IWC Hamburg

It is especially the different themes in the presentations which create so much charm in the meetings for me

I was also asked to say a few words about my joining Inner Wheel and what motivates me to take part. But before I start I would like to say a few words about myself.

My name is Elisabeth Dörner, I am 39 years old and have been married for eight years. We have two children aged between one and three and another is underway. My oldest child is handicapped because of an exceptionally premature birth and now goes to a special educational nursery school

My husband and I moved to Hamburg in 2007. Previously we had studied and worked in Frankfurt. My employer is still in Frankfurt. I am currently on maternity leave or to put it another way I am a full time mother and housewife.

I have known Rotary since my childhood as friends of my parents were members and a young New Zealander lived with us for several months as part of a Rotary exchange programme. This induced me to become active in Rotaract during my period as a banking trainee in Bielefeld, at least for a short period.

I first learnt about Inner Wheel from by mother in law Elke Dörner, who always told me about her Inner Wheel activities with pleasure and enthusiasm.

But it was only after we came to Hamburg about three years ago that I took more interest in the club life of Inner Wheel. Another factor was that I had also met several friends from my mother in law's Hamburg club.

But it was Luzia Hagenmüller who brought me to Inner Wheel.

She organised a tea afternoon for young Inner Wheelers and young ladies who could have interest in becoming members. Luzia invited some young Inner Wheelers from the IWC Hamburg to the pleasant tea along with those interested in joining. After a stimulating round of conversations in this "safe" environment among like-minded people of the same age, I learned more about Inner Wheel and also something about its structures.

It was the monthly meetings which attracted me to remain. After the tea afternoon I attended several meetings with themes which interested me and I found it very stimulating to take part.

That is why I have now been a member of the Inner Wheel Club Hamburg for two years.

This is what I would like to say about this:
I found and find that as a housewife and mother that you very quickly speak about nothing else except children and cooking etc and it is hard to break out of this cycle. Naturally these are many-sided themes in which there is always something to talk about – perhaps like the weather. But it is easy, especially as the mother of a handicapped child, to withdraw into your own ivory tower. You tend to focus only on your very own "challenges" and it is difficult to break out of the enclosed circle.

In addition you have a huge amount of work to do and it is hard to find the time even to read a newspaper.

This is where Inner Wheel can provide a wonderful gain. On the one side there is the chance to talk about something else other than the children. On the other hand you can gain knowledge about other subjects and have a chance to hear about issues and themes which are new to you.

I also have the experience that it is really always possible to keep one afternoon per month free so that you can break out of your old pattern.

The meetings were and are time and again an enrichment for me. This community of like-minded friends. The cordial atmosphere in the afternoon meetings are always worth the time that you invest in them.

Time and again it is the speeches and presentations which have much to offer. They cover a wide spectrum, depending on the local president. In a short time I have heard speeches about culture (presentation about a famous artist), social (presentation about a children's museum), judicial (about the new divorce law), business (the tea industry) and the Internet (newspapers in the 21st century). A discussion about the presentation and its background is also a part of the meeting.

It is especially the different themes in the presentations which create so much charm in the meetings for me

These are also hours which pull me out of my normal daily routine. This also means that, for example, you start to get dressed up again. But I also value above all the opportunity to think about different subjects. You hear that there are so many themes in the world to interest you.

Unfortunately, I still seldom have enough time to take part in all the other continuing activities. But I hope the time will come. My time in the club is after all not about to come to an end.

Here is a tip in this connection: Mothers often have more time in the mornings when the children are in nursery schools and/or at school. This means activities which take place in the mornings or at a more child-orientated time are easier for us to organise – or at least give us the chance to take part.

I am, for example, trying to participate again in our annual bazaar preparations and I also plan to actively participate in the sales.

I find the club life stimulating and it gives me a lot of fun, even if I cannot take part in all the events. But I have one ace up my sleeve: my mother in law. She has been a member since the club was established, knows how Inner Wheel works and also takes part in many activities.

I often hear that someone is seeking to persuade their daughter/daughter in law to join Inner Wheel and what my advice is. I can simply recommend they join!

Especially as a "young member" you will probably not have so much time or you will not be familiar with the organisation's structures. So an experienced "friend" can be very helpful.
My mother in law, for example, often tells me what happened during the various activities which I could not participate in. A special example of this was the "Rallye Charlemagne" which she told me and the rest of the club about with great enthusiasm.

This also brings me closer to my mother in law. My relationship to her always was and is good. But undertaking something together promotes communication and is a great gain for both of us. Even my husband perhaps feels a little left out when we talk so enthusiastically about Inner Wheel.

However, I would like to thank Luzia once more for the good idea and good organisation of the tea afternoon. This gave my wish to join Inner Wheel a powerful push. I received the feeling that I was welcome when I attended the following meetings and had the feeling that I already knew others there.

I hope I have been able to give a small insight into the motivation which led me to Inner Wheel. I also hope that my example will motivate others to join Inner Wheel and to participate in club life.

Appendix

What is Inner Wheel

„Inner Wheel concentrates upon friendship and personal service. It is not what is termed 'a money raising organisation' but each Club selects its own charities and channels of service.
One of the greatest features of Inner Wheel is the opportunity given to members the world over to get to know one another, thus contributing to international friendship and understanding.
International Conventions are held at intervals – any member may attend and Rotarians are always welcome.

International Inner Wheel

International Inner Wheel links together members in Clubs in countries from Europe to Africa, India, the Philippines, Australia, New Zealand, the United States of America and Canada – to name but a few.
Members are able to communicate with one another through correspondence, exchange visits, and joining together in international projects. Presidential tours bring members close together as they learn of Inner Wheel activities in vastly different territories. Clubs give service in their own communities as well as looking beyond their national boundaries.
In order to appreciate fully the strength and traditions of Inner Wheel, one must of course, look back at the inspiration, devotion and vision of our Founder President and those who have given such fine leadership over the years.
The roots from which International Inner Wheel has grown were established in 1934 when the Association of Inner Wheel Clubs in Great Britain and Ireland was formed with Mrs. Oliver Golding as the Founder President and Mrs. Nixon as Secretary, both being members of the Manchester Club which was formed in England in 1924. They realised that unity is strength and had the wisdom and foresight first, to group Clubs in Districts and then, later to bring the Districts together to form an Association.
At an early stage in its existence Inner Wheel began to spread overseas, Ballarat (Australia), Berger (Norway), Napier (New Zealand), Winnipeg (Canada), and Port Elizabeth (South Africa), being among the first Clubs formed. In 1947 the words 'in Great Britain and Ireland' were removed from the title and it became known as the 'Association of Inner Wheel Clubs'.
In 1962 for the first time members from countries outside Great Britain and Ireland were invited to sit on the Governing Body, but it was not until 1967

when International Inner Wheel came into being that there was the opportunity for qualified members in any country to become Officers, for example, President...." [1]

Emblem [2]

Website: www.internationalinnerwheel.org

1),2) International Inner Wheel Constitution and Handbook 2009, Staffort Court, Washway Road, Sale, Cheshire, M33 7PE, UK
Printed in England by Raisprint Dixon Target, Royd Way, Keighley, West Yorkshire, BD21 3LG –
Page: 34, 35, 1

www.ingramcontent.com/pod-product-compliance
Ingram Content Group UK Ltd.
Pitfield, Milton Keynes, MK11 3LW, UK
UKHW040642060526
12295UKWH00010B/30